An Elf for Christmas

MICHAEL GARLAND

DUTTON CHILDREN'S BOOKS
NEW YORK

To Katie, Alice, and Kevin

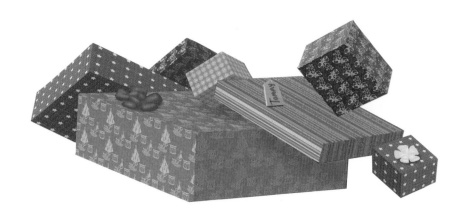

Library of Congress Cataloging-in-Publication Data

Garland, Michael, date.
An elf for Christmas / by Michael Garland.—1st ed.
p.   cm.
Summary: After falling asleep and being delivered along with
a toy airplane for Christmas, a hard-working elf tries
to make his way back to the North Pole.
ISBN 0-525-46212-0 (hc)
[1. Elves—Fiction. 2. Christmas—Fiction.] I. Title.
PZ7.G18413E1   1999   [E]—dc21   99-12259   CIP

Published in the United States 1999 by Dutton Children's Books,
a division of Penguin Putnam Books for Young Readers
345 Hudson Street, New York, New York 10014
http://www.penguinputnam.com/yreaders/index.htm

Designed by Sarah Massimo
Art direction by Rick Farley

Printed in Hong Kong   First Edition
1 3 5 7 9 10 8 6 4 2

The North Pole wind whipped the night air outside Santa's workshop, but the elf named Hieronimus Tingle was too busy to notice. Tingle, which is what everyone called him, was hard at work tightening the wheels on each toy airplane that came down the assembly line. Although Tingle was only one elf among many, he liked to think of himself as the best of Santa's workers. That night he had worked longer and harder than any of the other elves. He loved his job and wanted Santa to be proud of him.

On this busy Christmas Eve, the whole workshop was filled with the noise of hammering, sawing, and sanding. Teams of elves painted and stitched, glued and carved, rushing to finish the toys that Santa would deliver. The clock had already struck eleven, and the gifts still had to be wrapped and loaded onto the sleigh.

Tingle installed the steering controls on the very last plane of the year.

This plane looks so real! he said to himself. *I think it's the best one we've ever made.*

He climbed into the cockpit and sat down to admire his work. Though Tingle felt proud and happy, every part of his little body ached with tiredness. He closed his eyes to rest for just a moment. Instead he fell into a deep sleep.

Beep, beep, beeeeeep! The departure buzzer blared through the workshop.

The last toy plane moved down the assembly line to the wrapping department, where it was hoisted into a box. None of the elves noticed Tingle or heard his little elf snores as they closed the lid and wrapped up the box. They taped on a tag that said *Joey*, and then the present was piled onto Santa's sleigh.

As Tingle slept, he dreamed he was flying through the air, faster than any bird. It was a wonderful feeling, and it lasted for a long time—until suddenly the world started to shake. Tingle awoke to a roar of ripping paper and tearing cardboard.

"Where am I? What's going on? Why is it so dark?" he whispered.

Then the lid of the box came off. Tingle couldn't believe his eyes. Staring back at him was the huge, grinning face of a real, live boy.

"Wow! Look at this neat plane from Santa!" the boy said to his family. "It even has a toy elf pilot! I wonder if this thing can really fly."

Tingle sat up stiffly in the seat of the plane, too afraid to move or speak.

Who are all of these people? he wondered. *What is this place?*

Before Tingle could answer his own questions, the boy pressed the start button behind the cockpit. The engine buzzed and the propeller whirled. When the boy let go, the plane arced across the room. The dog went leaping and barking after it. Tingle hung on, keeping his eyes closed. Before long, the plane crashed into the Christmas tree. Tingle tumbled through the branches onto the floor. The boy ran over and picked him up. Tingle felt dizzy, but he just held his breath, staring straight ahead.

"Be careful, Joey," his mother warned. "Put that toy pilot in a safe place until you finish opening your other presents. He's so tiny—someone might step on him."

Joey climbed up on a chair and placed Tingle way up high on a bookshelf. From his perch, Tingle could see everyone and everything. Whimpering and growling, the dog stared suspiciously up at the little elf.

Tingle spent the whole day silently pretending to be a toy and watching the family enjoy their Christmas together. He had never felt so homesick and alone.

I've got to get back to the North Pole! he thought.

When the family finally went to bed and the dog was peacefully snoring, Tingle allowed himself to move. He slumped down against the bookshelf and stretched his aching legs.

I know I can't bother Santa, Tingle thought. *After his big night, he always takes a long nap. No, I'll have to find a way home on my own.*

Then it came to him—a wonderful, magical idea. "I'll fly home!" he whispered. Carefully, Tingle climbed down from the shelf and tiptoed past the sleeping dog.

Tingle gazed proudly at the plane he had helped build. He had seen how the boy had made it fly.

I'll just have to figure out how to steer, Tingle thought. *How hard could it be?*

He hopped into the plane, studied the control panel, then reached back and pushed the start button. The engine hummed, the propeller whirred, and the plane took off into the air.

The dog woke up. Barking wildly, he nipped and jumped at the circling plane. Tingle worried that the dog would wake the family. But then a bigger worry seized him—he had forgotten that it was winter and all the doors and windows in the house were shut! "How will I ever get out?" Tingle moaned.

The dog kept barking, louder and louder. Before long, Tingle saw Joey clumping down the stairs. The plane dipped and turned. Tingle did his best to keep it steady, but it wasn't easy. As Tingle flew around the room once more and swerved toward the fireplace, he had an idea. He would get out the same way Santa got in!

Tingle experimented with flying the plane. After a while, he began to feel more like a real pilot.

Flying is a little more difficult than I thought, but I'm beginning to get the hang of it, he said to himself. He did a few barrel rolls just for fun.

It was thrilling to see the world from so high up. But, looking down at the wide expanse of earth, Tingle had a moment of panic.

How do I know if I'm flying in the right direction? Then he remembered. *I live at the North Pole! I can just go north by following the plane's compass.*

Tingle settled back to enjoy the changing scenery. The plane passed over little towns and glittering cities, fields and forests, and then nothing but small islands floating in the sea.

After a long time, Tingle dropped down below the clouds to see if he could spot anything familiar. He smiled when he saw ice and snow. He knew he must be getting close to home.

Tingle's stomach began to growl. He pictured the Christmas dinner he had missed at the North Pole, the table heaped with delicious food, hot from Mrs. Claus's oven. He missed celebrating with the other elves.

Does anyone even know I'm gone? he wondered.

Before he could worry any more, the battery warning light suddenly flashed on.

"Oh no, I'm losing power!" shrieked Tingle.

The engine made a sputtering sound. The propeller slowed, and the plane began a nosedive—down, down, down. As the wind rushed past his face, there was nothing Tingle could do but hold on tight.

The plane plummeted from the sky and plowed with a *whooshhh!* into a snowdrift. A big cloud of snow rose into the air, and then there was silence.

Tingle wriggled his fingers and wiggled his toes. He was glad to find he was all in one piece.

What am I going to do now? he said to himself. *The North Pole must still be a long way off.*

He looked down at the broken compass, and then out at the miles and miles of snow and ice.

"I'll never get home now," he said sadly.

He was still staring into the distance when the snowdrift under him started to move.

It was no snowdrift. It was an enormous napping polar bear!

"Oh, how do I get myself into so much trouble?" groaned Tingle.

But he needn't have worried. The polar bear just chuckled and lowered his head so that Tingle could slide to the ground.

Realizing the bear was friendly, Tingle quickly explained who he was and what had happened to him. The bear listened carefully and then nodded. "You are still a long way from home, but Santa is a good friend of mine. I would be happy to help you get back to the North Pole."

At last, they reached Santa's workshop. As Tingle slid to the ground, the door burst open and Santa, Mrs. Claus, and all the elves spilled out.

"Hurrah! Tingle is back!" they shouted. "Welcome home, Tingle!"

The elves gave the bear some fish and thanked him for helping their friend. Then Tingle went inside to enjoy the Christmas dinner they had saved for him. In between bites, he told the elves his tale of daring adventure.

"I'm proud of you, Tingle," said Santa. "I knew you wouldn't forget our old saying, 'If there's no one around to help an elf, an elf should help himself.'"

"You've had a very busy Christmas," Santa said. "Why don't you go on to bed and get some sleep."

"Soon," said Tingle. "But right now there's *one* more thing I have to do."

Santa's Workshop
North Pole

Dear Joey,

We here at Santa's Workshop apologize for any inconvenience the recall of your toy plane might have caused. I hope you enjoy the new replacement.

Merry Christmas!

Hieronimus Jingle